Worried
Little Lamb

A Little Animal Adventure

Worried Little Lamb

Written by Valérie Guidoux
Adapted by Patricia Jensen
Illustrations by Geneviève Monjaret

Published by The Reader's Digest Association Limited
London ❖ New York ❖ Sydney ❖ Montreal

One fine day, a flock of sheep who all lived together in the French Alps were going out onto the slopes to graze on the new spring grass. 'Come along,' Mother called to Little Lamb, who was playing with some butterflies. 'It's time for your first trip up the mountain.'

'I'm coming,' said Little Lamb.

Mischievous Marmot, a furry little mountain animal, was hiding nearby and heard their conversation.

'Little Lamb is going to the mountains for the first time,' he chuckled. 'I know how my friend Rabbit and I can have some fun.'

Marmot called to Little Lamb. 'My friend Rabbit and I have been on the mountain many times. To get there, you have to climb up and down some very steep slopes. Poor Little Lamb! You'll never be able to do it.'

'Why not?' she asked.

'Well your legs aren't strong enough,' said Marmot. 'You'll probably stumble and tumble all the way to the bottom.'

Little Lamb was very young and believed almost everything she heard.

'Oh, my,' said Little Lamb, her eyes wide with fright.

Little Lamb raced after the flock of sheep and found Grandma.

'Grandma,' she asked. 'Do I have to go up and down steep slopes to get to the mountain?'

'Yes, you do,' answered Grandma.

'Oh, no,' Little Lamb said in a shaky voice. 'I won't be able to do it. My legs aren't strong enough.'

Grandma smiled. 'You won't know until you try, Little Lamb. Besides, your mother certainly wouldn't lead you to a place you couldn't reach. We will all be there to help you.'

But Little Lamb was still worried when she caught up with Grandpa.

'Grandpa,' she said, 'I am afraid that my legs are too weak to carry me up the mountain.'

Grandpa snorted. 'Your legs are plenty strong enough. You'll have no trouble at all. Besides, your mother and grandmother and I will be there to help you.'

Little Lamb climbed on munching the tasty grass along the way but then the ground suddenly stopped! Little Lamb peered over the edge and saw how steep it was the other side.

'Oh, no!' she thought. 'This is much too steep. Marmot and Rabbit were right – I will never be able to climb down! I'll stumble and tumble all the way to the bottom!'

Little Lamb's mother found her daughter and said, 'We're almost there.'

'But, Mother,' cried Little Lamb. 'I can't climb down such a steep slope. My legs are much too weak.'

'Where did you ever get that idea?' asked her surprised mother.

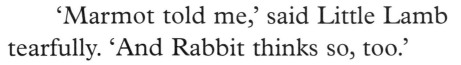

'Marmot told me,' said Little Lamb
tearfully. 'And Rabbit thinks so, too.'

'You'll never know what you can do until
you try,' Mother said gently. 'And we're all here
to help you.'

Little Lamb's mother began to lead the way.
Little Lamb took a deep breath, and then she
took one careful step and another and another.

Little Lamb climbed all the way down slowly and carefully. Marmot and Rabbit were waiting at the bottom.

Little Lamb's mother went over to the two rascals. 'You have been mean to Little Lamb today,' she scolded. 'You should not have told her that she wouldn't be able to climb down the slope. It was not too steep for her.'

'We were only kidding,' said Marmot, hanging his head in shame.

'Playing tricks on your friends is not a good way to have fun,' Mother said firmly.

'We're sorry,' said Marmot.

Little Lamb's mother smiled as Little Lamb played in the meadow with Rabbit, Marmot and all their brothers and sisters.

'I've learnt how to find out things for myself,' Little Lamb said to Marmot. 'So no one will be able to trick me again. And I know now that my legs are strong. In fact, they are so strong, I can give you all a ride!'

And that's just
what Little
Lamb did.

All about ... LAMBS

EWES AND RAMS
Female sheep are called ewes and male sheep are called rams. Sheep live together in flocks and graze on grass.

WARM WOOLLIES
Most sheep live in flocks on farmland. Their wool is used to make warm sweaters and blankets. Their milk is used to make cheese.

FACT FILE
HEAD LOCKS
All wild rams have horns. When they fight, they knock against each other and butt with their horns.

Did know?

FLEECED

Sheep have their woolly coats, called fleeces, shorn in the warm weather. Being shorn is like getting a hair cut. The wool grows back.

SPRING LAMBS

Lambs are usually born in late spring. They drink their mother's milk until they are about four months old. Then they can graze by themselves.

LUSH SLOPES

Especially in Europe, flocks of sheep are led to the mountains each spring. All summer long they graze on the tender grass produced by mountain rains.

Worried Little Lamb is a Little Animal Adventures book
published by Reader's Digest Young Families, Inc.

Written by Valérie Guidoux
Adapted by Patricia Jensen
Illustrations by Geneviève Monjaret
Notebook artwork © Paul Bommer

This edition was adapted and published in 2008 by
The Reader's Digest Association Limited
11 Westferry Circus, Canary Wharf, London E14 4HE

We are committed both to the quality of our products
and the service we provide to our customers.
We value your comments, so please do contact us on
08705 113366 or via our website at
www.readersdigest.co.uk
If you have any comments or suggestions about the
content of our books, email us at
gbeditorial@readersdigest.co.uk

Printed in China

Book code: 637-041 UP0000-1
ISBN: 978 0 276 44368 8
Oracle code: 501800111H.00.24